Jan 2013

Carol E. Sandau

Dear Marylin
I hope you enjoy the
story —
Smiles
Carol

Prairie Patchwork

Carol E. Sandau

iUniverse, Inc.
Bloomington

Prairie Patchwork

iUniverse books may be ordered through booksellers or by contacting:

iUniverse
1663 Liberty Drive
Bloomington, IN 47403
www.iuniverse.com
1-800-Authors (1-800-288-4677)

Because of the dynamic nature of the Internet, any web addresses or links contained in this book may have changed since publication and may no longer be valid. The views expressed in this work are solely those of the author and do not necessarily reflect the views of the publisher, and the publisher hereby disclaims any responsibility for them.

Any people depicted in stock imagery provided by Thinkstock are models, and such images are being used for illustrative purposes only.

Certain stock imagery © Thinkstock.

ISBN: 978-1-4759-4807-3 (sc)
ISBN: 978-1-4759-4808-0 (e)

Printed in the United States of America

iUniverse rev. date: 9/12/2012

Acknowledgements

I would like to extend thanks and appreciation to a number of people who have assisted me during this creative process.

Since early childhood days, pioneer life has always held a special attraction for me. Of course I did research on the subject and had my ears open to various stories I heard over the years. However, the completion of this novel was due to input from many other sources.

The seed for writing this story was planted a few years ago when my six grandchildren: Zach, Joel, Matty, Shayleen, Miranda and Luke, were younger. Having them living nearby provided plenty of insight and inspiration regarding the actions of children.

My husband, Lloyd, was my support and provided interesting insights about farm life from his own personal experiences.

Daughter Melanie was my computer expert, easily guiding me through some of the challenges in this area.

Daughter Cathy, who is a teacher, provided early suggestions which helped enhance a few areas that needed tweaking.

Louise patiently edited the manuscript and Miranda proofread it again.

Most importantly, thanks to God for this gift he has graciously bestowed on me.

Also by Carol E. Sandau

~ ~ ~ ~ ~ ~

Timeless Treasures (Poetry)

10 Puzzling Pieces

For my family and friends who supported me on this journey.

Prologue

The early pioneers packed their belongings and boarded ships. Many of them came from various parts of Europe to pursue their dream. The trip was very long and difficult. Most were weakened with long bouts of sea sickness on the journey over. Finally after weeks of travel, they arrived on the eastern shores of America where they gathered to form wagon trains.

These brave souls were seeking a new life. Various stories had spread about how they could obtain land at low cost on the wide open spaces out west. They were planning to homestead there.

Covered wagons were often the way to travel. Usually groups of 20 to 40 wagons travelled together for safety. Even so it was a long, often dangerous journey with many mishaps along the way. Due to sickness and accidents countless people lost their lives on the trail.

The wagon was tented with a large rounded tarp to protect household items, food, medical supplies they were taking to their new home. Furniture was also strapped on, but in many cases had to be discarded during the long trip.

Horses, mules or oxen pulled the wagons. Able family members walked beside the wagon to lighten the load. A wagon master led the group and guided them on the trip. The wagons were formed into a circle at night for protection from weather, thieves and predators.

Once they arrived at their chosen location, the family would leave the group to clear and settle their piece of land. A sod house, made from squares of grass that were cut, stacked on top of each other, glued with mud and set into a hillside, became their first home. Later they would use logs or lumber to construct a small house.

Thus started a life of adventure on the windswept prairies. The work would be difficult; hard work and loneliness would be a constant companion. Even though neighbors were a great distance away, they always helped each other out and got together for celebrations.

The Robertson's were only one of the many families who travelled west to become settlers.

Chapter 1

A cloud of dust streaked across the windswept prairie. Suddenly it came to an abrupt halt. As the gritty dirt settled a horse and rider were revealed. The small jean clad figure slid off the sweating red pony. A thick braid trailing down her back betrayed the fact the slight form was a girl.

Katy ran lightly up the rickety plank steps and into the kitchen. The squeaky screen door banged shut behind her.

"Ma! Ma! Where are you?" she yelled.

The house was strangely quiet. Her sisters, nine year old Sarah and three year old Rebecca were sitting at the kitchen table playing with two well-worn rag dolls. Sara looked up. Her sad brown eyes welled with tears.

"Mama's real sick, Katy," she said softly. "She wants you to go see her right away."

Katy crossed swiftly into the bedroom next door only a few feet away. Her exhausted mother lay on the bed with a tiny red-faced baby in her arms.

"Katy, I'm so glad you're here," her mother whispered gently. "Meet your new baby brother, Jacob."

"I'm so sorry, dear," Mother continued weakly. "I don't think I can go on. I'm very, very tired."

Gently squeezing Katy's hand in her own limp one, she made her final request.

"Promise me you'll look after the family for me. I love all of you very much."

"Oh, Ma, please get better," Katy sobbed. "We need you."

She knew it was already too late. Her mother's eyes fluttered shut and with a final breath she was completely still.

"Yes, Ma, I'll try to do my best," Katy murmured quietly. Brushing her sorrow aside, Katy swiped at the tears on her cheeks.

Jacob, sensing something wrong, howled in protest. Katy quickly scooped the crying baby into her arms and wrapped him in a towel. She covered her mother's lifeless body with a blanket.

Katy walked slowly into the kitchen and laid the baby on the table.

"Sarah, Rebecca, this is your new baby brother, Jacob," she announced.

She crouched between the two sisters and put her arms around them.

"Mama was very sick. She's gone to heaven," she said gently. Katy hugged the two sobbing girls close to her.

"We'll have to be very strong and brave. Sarah, you can ride the pony over to the Bailey's place and tell them to come quick."

Katy was 13 years old and knew she was in charge of the house now. Her pa was away working at the logging camp earning money to make ends meet. He had put in the crop before he left in the spring.

Sarah ran out to the barn and jumped on Little Red. She rode bareback the five miles to the closest neighbour.

Mr. and Mrs. Bailey and their two boys, 15 year old Tommy and eleven year old Matthew soon arrived with their horses and wagon.

"You poor dears," the kindly Mrs. Bailey said. She wrapped her arms around the three sisters. "Don't be worrying. We'll help you get things sorted out."

Mr. Bailey and the two boys quickly constructed a coffin out of used lumber. They dug a grave on the hillside under a tree.

The two adults, five children and baby held a short funeral service with Mr. Bailey reading from the old family bible. Even Buster, the family dog, laid his head on his paws. Due to the unbearable heat, it was necessary to bury a body as soon as possible. To notify Pa and have him travel home would take a few days. He had planned on coming home in a month's time when the baby was due. However, the baby was born sooner than expected.

Mrs. Bailey offered to take Jacob to her house for the time being.

"I have some bottles and milk at my place so I can look after him for now. Since he was born early he is very small and will need extra care."

Katy agreed this would be a good idea. She knew she'd have enough problems trying to keep the household together. She had no idea how to care for a baby. Katy was often referred to as a tomboy.

Being the eldest in the family and with no brothers until now, she looked after doing the chores most times. She mended fences, milked the two cows, fed the pigs and retrieved eggs from the chickens. Katy rarely wore a dress. She preferred overalls or worn jeans which she found much more practical. Katy often pulled a weather-beaten old cowboy hat low on her head to protect it from the sun. She helped her father with the seeding in the spring and harvest in the fall. She tended the garden during the summer months.

"We'll have to be getting home now," Mrs. Bailey said. "Chores to do you know."

She picked a fussing Jacob up and rocked him gently. The boys, loaded down with the cradle, bedding, diapers and tiny clothes Ma had ready for the baby, ran out to the wagon.

"Come and get us if you need anything," Mrs. Bailey said, smiling at the three girls. "Tommy and Mr. Bailey will drop in now and then to see how you're doing."

"I'll see your pa knows what happened," Mr. Bailey added quietly. "I'm sure somebody will be heading west soon, so he can hook up with them. He clucked his tongue at the horses. The wagon rolled slowly down the rutted trail.

Chapter 2

Sighing softly, Katy dropped a chunk of wood into the burning fire.

"Sarah, you can heat that pot of stew for supper. I'm going out to milk the cows and tend to the other animals."

The sun had gone down in a blazing ball of fire in the western sky when Katy returned to the house. She poured two dippers full of water into the old tin basin and scrubbed vigorously at her hands and face.

Darkness was descending, so Katy lit the lantern. The girls were surprisingly hungry. They gulped the stew and mopped the juice up with hunks of crusty bread. After rinsing the bowls and forks, Katy blew out the lamp. The candle she carried provided a small circle of light as Katy herded the two younger girls into the second bedroom. This tiny room had only enough space for a double bed and a small dresser. After changing into their nightgowns, the three girls tumbled into the squeaky bed.

Rebecca started crying.

"I want my mama," she whimpered. The three sisters snuggled close together in their misery, huddled under the cozy down comforter.

~~~~~~~

The rooster crowed. Bright sunshine streamed through the small window onto the sleeping girls. Katy yawned and squeezed her eyes shut against the brilliant rays. Mid-stretch she remembered with a sharp pang. Ma was gone and Pa wasn't home yet.

No time to dawdle. She was in charge now and had to get busy.

"Sarah, help Rebecca get dressed," Katy instructed. "I'll get the fire going and start the chores. You can stir up some porridge for breakfast." Sarah was the one who helped Ma in the house.

Katy's only experience with the old cook stove was to add a stick of wood now and then to build the flames up. Ma or Pa had always started it.

She crumpled some paper and added wood. Katy lit a match and threw it into the cold stove. Nothing happened. She struck another match, threw it in, and stirred at it with the poker. She jammed the lid on. Still nothing. Katy took the lid off again. This time heavy gray smoke billowed out and soon filled the tiny cabin. Coughing and choking, Katy grabbed her two sputtering sisters and ran outside.

With the door open, the gray fumes finally cleared out of the house. The girls went back inside and ate a cold breakfast of bread smeared with Ma's homemade blueberry jam.

Katy went about doing the chores.

"Sarah, you can feed the chickens and collect eggs. Take Rebecca with you."

Later in the day, Mr. Bailey rode in to check on the girls. Mr. Bailey was usually a man of few words.

"Brought some cooked sausage and biscuits. Guess you have plenty of milk and butter. Berries are 'bout ready for picking. Your garden's growing good."

Mr. Bailey chuckled when he heard the tale of the stubborn stove. He gave the two older girls a lesson on starting a fire in the stove.

"Always remember to open the chimney damper before you start. That allows air to come in and fan the fumes." He demonstrated this for the girls.

"With the damper closed the fire will smother itself," he explained.

"I sent word with ol' Oscar to let your Pa know what happened here," Mr. Bailey continued. "Your Pa should be coming home soon."

Chapter 3

It was Saturday afternoon.

"Sarah, its bath night. Let's start hauling pails of water from the well," Katy said as she banged out the screen door. "We'll heat water on the stove like Ma did."

Katy and Sarah struggled as they dragged the tin washtub in. They filled it with the warm water from the reservoir on the stove. Rebecca, being the youngest, was first in line for a bath. Then it was Sarah's turn. Finally, Katy scrubbed herself. When they were finished, the two girls tugged the heavy tub slowly across the floor and dumped it outside.

Sunday dawned sunny and cloudless.

"Sarah, you can get you and Rebecca dressed in your Sunday best. The Bailey's are dropping by to take us to church."

The girls climbed into the Bailey's wagon. Baby Jacob seemed to be very content as he lay tightly wrapped in a blanket on Mrs. Bailey's lap. It was good to go to town and see their friends.

After church, the little group stopped at the Bailey's place for a big dinner of fried chicken, potatoes and mashed turnips and biscuits. Bread pudding completed the meal. Soon everyone was stuffed and happy.

The children went outside to play "Kick the Can" and "Hide and Seek." Mrs. Bailey bundled up some leftover food and Tommy drove the girls home in the wagon. They all agreed it was a fun day. It helped them forget their sorrow for awhile.

Next morning, the bright fiery ball of sun rising in the east promised another sweltering day.

"Sarah, it's Monday, you'll need to pack a lunch and ride Little Red to school this morning," Katy said. "Tell Miss Holmes I can't come. I'll have to stay home with Rebecca and look after things here."

Sarah fed the chickens and collected the eggs. She got some porridge stirred up. The two older girls now had the knack of firing up the old cook stove. Sarah grabbed the lard pail that contained her lunch, ran outside and jumped on the pony.

"Bye, Katy. Bye, Becky, see you later."

Rebecca spent the day clutching her little rag doll and following Katy around as she worked. In the afternoon, Katy was busy weeding the garden. Rebecca was playing on the porch.

"Here, Kitty, nice Kitty," she crooned softly.

A startled Katy looked up.

"Becky, don't touch!" she shouted. "Come here, fast!" Rebecca obeyed and ran to her sister.

Katy shuddered. "Rebecca that was a skunk. See the white stripe down his back? He would spray you and make you stink if you touched him."

"Tinky kitty, tinky kitty," Rebecca giggled.

"I'm sure glad you didn't touch him." Katy hugged her little sister.

~~~~~~~

Later in the day twin swirls of twisting dust announced the arrival of Mr. Bailey and Tommy. They slid of their sweat soaked horses and walked toward Katy who was still weeding in the garden.

"Mrs. Bailey sent this along for your supper."

Mr. Bailey presented a pot still warm from the stove. Biscuits were wrapped in a checkered towel stacked on top.

"Thank you very much," Katy smiled. "Your family is so good to us."

Tommy appeared to be hiding something behind his back and he shuffled his feet awkwardly.

"Okay, son, you can show her," Mr. Bailey's quiet voice was a little gruff.

Tommy looked shyly at Katy as he handed her his offering. It was two pieces of wood nailed together to form a cross. The letters M.E.R. had been carved on the front.

"Those are Ma's initials," Katy exclaimed. "Mary Elizabeth Robertson was her name."

"Yeah, Pa and me will pound it in over your Ma's gravesite. We thought you girls can go and visit whenever you feel lonely and need to "talk" to your Ma."

Katy nodded her head while unshed tears pooled in her deep blue eyes. The two men trudged down the hill to do their chore.

After school next day, Katy, Sarah and Rebecca wandered down to the gravesite. It was located in the far corner of the field under one of the few trees on the property. Along the way, the girls picked crocuses and other wild flowers.

Arriving at the site, they found Mr. Bailey and Tommy had hammered the cross in at the head of the grave. They had also placed rocks outlining the slightly raised mound on the ground. The three girls threw the odd assortment of flowers over the freshly turned dirt, creating a colorful blanket. Satisfied with their display they sat on the ground in a small semi-circle. In soft whispers Katy, Sarah and Rebecca each took turns "visiting" with their mother for awhile. Sometimes a few tears were shed.

On the way back to the house, Sarah stopped suddenly. She looked at her sisters.

"I know Mama wasn't really there, but somehow I feel better after that little visit."

"You're right, Sarah" Katy replied slowly. "I feel the same way. Sometimes it just feels good to chat about things a little. Now we know we can go there whenever we need to talk about what's bothering us."

Rebecca giggled and nodded her head as she skipped up the hill.

~~~~~~~

It was Friday afternoon near the middle of June. The day was once again burning hot. Katy was hauling pails of water to pour on the dry, cracked ground of the garden. Rebecca was sitting in the shade near the panting dog. She was piling little rocks into different shapes.

A sharp sound in the distance caused Katy to look up abruptly. She shielded her eyes as she squinted into the bright sun. A lazy dust formation was slowly trailing across the western horizon toward them. As the slumped figure came into view, Rebecca clapped her hands.

"Papa, Papa!" she exclaimed happily.

Pa slid slowly off his horse. Holding a navy dotted hanky to his mouth he burst into a fit of coughing. Finally he caught his breath.

"Pa, what's wrong?" a frightened Katy asked.

"Got the message about your Ma a few days ago," Pa answered slowly. "I've been feeling poorly. Went to see Doc Brown. He says I have something called tuberculosis. Says I have to go to a place called a sanitarium in the city to get better. Have to stay away from folks for awhile and take medicine."

"But, Pa," Katy asked fearfully, "What will happen to us?"

"I guess you'll have to carry on best you can," Pa answered sadly. "Neighbours can help some."

The words hung heavy in the still air. Grasshoppers were chirping in the field, flies were buzzing around them. Everything was the same, but now so different.

Sarah came galloping toward them on Little Red. Following close behind was Miss Lydia Holmes, the community teacher. She'd been coming out every so often to help Katy with her lessons.

"Papa!Papa! I'm so glad you're home," a happy Sarah squealed as she threw herself into Pa's outstretched arms.

"I'm mighty pleased to see all you girls, too," Pa responded. "I'm just sorry I have to be leaving right away."

Katy filled Sarah and Miss Holmes in on Pa's sickness.

"I think I might have an idea that could help some," Miss Holmes said thoughtfully. "I have a friend who lives in the city. She's been staying home looking after her sick parents the last few years. Her mom and dad both passed away recently. Anna's wanted to come out here and start over. Maybe she could live with you and look after the house."

Pa thought that sounded like a good idea.

"I'll send a message to Anna as soon as I can and let you know," Miss Holmes continued.

Pa left early next morning. Now that Pa's horse Sam was back, they had a team to hitch to the wagon. Katy knew how to drive so the three girls took Pa to town where he would catch a ride to the city.

"I know you can look after things," Pa said. "Katy, girl, you'll have to be in charge. Soon as I'm better I'll be back. Doc figures it may be a year."

"Bye, Papa, we'll miss you," the sisters chorused tearfully.

Pa walked away slowly with his head lowered so they would not see the unshed tears in his eyes.

~~~~~~~

On one of her trips out to the farm in late June, Miss Holmes jumped from her horse before it was fully stopped.

"Hi, girls," she grinned cheerfully. "I just got a note from Anna. She said she'll be real happy to come and stay with you for awhile."

"That's good news," Katy smiled. "How soon is she coming?"

"She needs some time to sort things out at home," Miss Holmes answered. "She thinks maybe she can catch a ride with a group of wagons heading this way in early September."

"Oh, yes," Miss Holmes continued. "I wanted to remind all of you to come to the picnic on Sunday after church."

"We'll be happy to come," Katy responded.

"By the way," Miss Holmes added. "I was talking to Mrs. Bailey. She said to tell you she'll bring plenty of food for your family as well as hers. She wondered if you could bring two jars of your Ma's delicious pickles she put up last year."

"That is so nice of Mrs. Bailey," Katy responded. "I'll get the pickles from the cold room and bring them along. See you then."

Sunday dawned bright and cloudless. Katy hurried with the chores. The two younger girls had eaten and were dressed for church. They grabbed blankets and the pickles and climbed into the wagon for the trip to town.

After the church service was over, everyone moved outside. The ladies set food on the makeshift tables. They were soon loaded with a selection of ham, chicken, potato salad, pickles and buns. Cakes, cookies and pies completed the feast.

Blankets were set out to sit on. The congregation joined the pastor in reciting the common prayer. Finally it was time to dig into heaping plates of food.

"Katy, Sarah, come join us. We're going to have a ball game," Tommy and Matt shouted from the hastily set up ball diamond. The younger children played ring around Rosie and tag, happy to have friends to run and play with.

Suddenly there were loud screams and shouts from the ball field. The always mischievous Johnny had found a snake and couldn't resist temptation. The snake was dangling from a stick and he was chasing the girls with it. The shrieks rang shrilly across the prairie. Finally it was dislodged and slithered into the grass.

Chapter 4

Katy ran lightly into the kitchen one hot afternoon in July.

"Sarah, Rebecca," she laughed happily. "I think it's finally going to rain."

The light fluffy clouds of early morning had melded together. Ominous black thunderheads were hanging low on the horizon. Suddenly a brilliant streak of lightning pierced the darkened sky. A huge drumroll of thunder shook the little house before echoing away on a westward path. Katy comforted a crying Rebecca who was frightened by the dramatic display. Fat raindrops started pattering on the roof top.

"Wait inside," Katy instructed her two sisters. "I'm going to put the animals in the shelter." She grabbed Pa's old slicker and raced out the door.

A minute later Katy ran back into the house.

"Come quick, girls," she screamed. "A fire has started in the hay from the lightning! Grab a pail, Sarah and start scooping water out of the horse trough."

Katy snatched gunny sacks and towels. She soaked them with water.

"Rebecca, you can hit the sparks on the edge with the wet towel. She handed the little girl the dripping wet material.

The three girls worked feverishly. Katy pounded the flames with the back of a shovel. Suddenly the rain started gushing down in torrents. It sizzled as it hit the leaping orange flames. Soon the fire was a smouldering mass of smoke, leaving a large black round scar beside the barn.

"We were so lucky the rain started," a breathless Katy gasped as she hugged her soot blackened sisters.

"Look as us. We look like spooks." Sarah and Rebecca giggled in nervous relief.

A few minutes later Mr. Bailey and Tommy, astride two rain-soaked horses, galloped into the yard. Water streamed off their black slickers.

"You girls okay?" Mr. Bailey inquired sharply.

"Y-yes," Katy stammered. "We had a fire, but got it out. The barn is still okay and all the animals are safe. We were very lucky."

"We figured the lightning might've hit nearby. Thought we'd better come and check on you." Mr. Bailey explained. "See you girls got it under control now. We'll come by tomorrow and make sure everything is alright."

The three shivering sisters ran into the house and stripped out of their soggy, wet clothes. They washed up and dried themselves with towels. The girls changed into their warm, cozy flannelette nighties and settled into bed for the night.

~~~~~~~

Mr. Bailey and Tommy came over the next day. Tommy was bursting with excitement.

"Big news," he enthused. "We just heard the fair is coming here in three weeks."

The carnival only came to town every five years, so it was a very big attraction.

"Katy, I've been thinking," Tommy continued. "You know they usually have horse races at the fair? What say you and me practice racing with our horses and enter the competition?"

"I think that would be fun," Katy agreed cheerfully. "It's not too busy on the farm right now, so I'd have time to practice with you."

"Good, I'll be over tomorrow morning," Tommy announced.

"See you then," Katy nodded.

So started a new routine for the two teenagers. They met every day for about an hour. Riding bareback they pitted their horses against each other. They ran the two horses as fast as they could down the road next to the pasture. Each day showed a little improvement in their speed. The mare and gelding were evenly matched and the competition was on.

"Hurry up, slow poke," Katy yelled at Tommy, egging him on. "Okay, smarty pants, I'll show you." Tommy slapped his horse on the rump and moved ahead.

"Gotcha," his words taunted.

The chummy rivalry continued between the two friends as they practiced over the next few weeks.

Chapter 5

Finally the big day arrived. Katy and Tommy rode their horses into town. The Bailey's came with their wagon and picked up Sara and Rebecca. The children wandered around the fairgrounds taking in all the sights. Ice cream was readily available and the children made sure they sampled as much as they could.

Various people were displaying and selling their wares. Saddles and tack for horses were mixed with pots and pans and dishes.

Over at the newly enclosed fairgrounds, demonstrations and competitions were taking place. Mrs. Bailey entered one of her famous pies in the contest, along with a dozen puffy white buns. Matt was showing one of his prize sheep. Mr. Bailey displayed his expertise in trick roping. Fiddlers were tuning their instruments preparing for a square dancing exhibition.

At 4 o'clock, the call came for the horse racing contestants to line up. Katy was in position number two; Tommy was number four out of six. Sidling up to Katy, Tommy leaned over.

"If I don't win, I sure want you to," he teased with a grin.

"That goes both ways," Katy countered. "Watch me go!"

"Three, two, one — they're off," the announcer declared.

Four horses jumped forward, two bolted sideways and were led off the track. Stretching out, Tommy's horse took the lead. Katy was behind by a length. At the three quarter point she had gained and her horse was neck and neck with Tommy's. A slap on Sam's hind quarters encouraged him forward. Katy and her horse, Sam, won the race by half a length.

The crowd was cheering wildly for the two finalists:

"Go, Katy. Go Tommy," they chanted.

"Sam, you are such a good boy," Katy whispered to the big horse. "I knew you could do it."

Once the horses were cooled down, Katy and Tommy were presented with red and blue ribbons.

"Congratulations, Katy," Tommy said proudly as he shook her hand.

"Thank you, Tommy," Katy replied quietly. "Remember you were my inspiration to try."

Chapter 6

September 2 dawned warm and sunny. Chores were done, the house tidied up and the girls were dressed in their Sunday best. They climbed into the wagon. Snapping the reins, Katy prodded the horses along. Arriving in town, the three sisters met Miss Holmes. They stood waiting in the shade by the general store.

Before long a huge plume of dust announced the arrival of eight wagons loaded with people and supplies. Men and women of various sizes and shapes jumped stiffly to the ground. Small children tumbled out, happy to be able to run around again. Infants were crying with the frustration of being confined for so long.

Out of the second wagon a small feminine figure emerged. Dressed in a long, pale blue floral dress, she stretched her travel stiffened limbs. Strands of bright red hair had escaped from the bun knotted at the nape of her neck. A smudge of dirt had settled on one rosy cheek. A limp sunbonnet hung loosely around her neck. It had long since been discarded from its original purpose of protecting her head from the sun's beating rays. Bright green eyes glittered as she surveyed the crowd. Anna had arrived!

Miss Holmes, catching sight of her friend ran toward her. "Oh, Anna, I'm so happy to see you," she said as she embraced her in a warm hug.

"Lydia," Anna replied, "I'm even happier to see you and be on solid ground again. That surely was a long trip."

"Come and meet the girls," Miss Holmes instructed softly. She made the introductions.

"Girls, I want you to meet my dear friend Anna. Anna, I'd like you to meet Katy, Sarah and Rebecca."

"We're pleased to meet you," the sisters replied shyly.

"I know we're going to have fun together," a smiling Anna announced cheerfully.

Two men lifted Anna's trunk down from the back of a wagon.

"Whew, that sure is heavy," a panting Clem grumbled. "Did you bring the kitchen stove with you, Ma'am?"

With a grunt, they heaved the cumbersome burden onto the back of the girls' wagon.

Anna lifted her skirt and hoisted herself up to the front seat beside Katy. Sarah and Rebecca settled themselves in back by the trunk.

"I'll come out and visit you all soon when you're settled," Miss Holmes informed them as she waved goodbye.

~~~~~~~

The Bailey's dropped by the next day to greet the newcomer. Mr. Bailey and Tommy struggled a little as they dragged the trunk into the corner of the parents' bedroom. Anna would be saying there until Pa returned.

The friendly Mrs. Bailey was chatting with Anna.

"Any help you need, just call on us," she advised.

She had brought some fresh baked bread with her. Anna was 26 years old and a city girl. She hadn't learned the art of baking and cooking. At home a hired lady had taken care of most of the household chores. With the assistance of a nurse, Anna helped look after her parents until their demise.

Mrs. Bailey was holding a squirming Jacob.

"I'll come over on Friday and show you how to do some things in the kitchen," she announced cheerfully. "It'll soon be harvest time and you'll have to feed a bunch."

"Thank you, Mrs. Bailey," a grateful Anna replied. "I'm sure not used to this kind of stove. I certainly need to learn about preparing meals."

"Anna, if you're comfortable with it, I'd be pleased if you'd call me Emma."

"Thanks, Emma, I look forward to Friday."

Chapter 7

The next day chores were done and breakfast finished quickly.

"Come on, girls, help me unpack my trunk," Anna requested as she bounced happily to the little room next door.

She raised the heavy lid to expose her treasures. The girls watched as Anna lifted out three cotton dresses in brilliant colors. Next came a long navy blue skirt and a ruffled white blouse, followed by some pretty lacy undergarments. The three sisters sat in wide-eyed wonder gazing at the beautiful clothes. Wrapped in a long white petticoat to protect it, was a pretty china doll.

"Rebecca, this is for you," Anna said. "She was mine when I was little and I want you to have her." The little girl happily cradled the doll in her arms.

The next item was wrapped in an ivory colored linen tablecloth. It was a small dainty teapot and two cups and saucers. Made of fine blue china, it had a pattern of tiny pink roses on it.

"Sarah, this belonged to my mother," Anna said gently. "I'd like you to have it."

"Ooh, it's so beautiful," Sarah enthused. "I'll look after it and keep it forever."

Finally Anna lifted up a square bundle of purple silk. Cautiously she unwrapped it revealing a gold watch on a long gold chain.

"Katy, this was a very special watch belonging to my father," Anna explained. "It's for you."

Katy couldn't believe her eyes. I will take very good care of it," she said as she carefully cupped the timepiece in her hands.

Reaching deeper into the trunk, Anna brought out three envelopes.

"These are flower seeds from our garden at home. Next spring we'll plant them so we can have colorful flowers by the house."

Now a square box appeared. It contained an assortment of needles, thread, thimbles, knitting needles, scissors, pins and everything necessary for sewing.

"I want to teach all of you how to sew, knit and embroider," Anna explained. "That will keep us busy during the long, cold winter I keep hearing about."

Underneath this were several swatches of material.

"I'm thinking these scraps of cotton can be used to make a big quilt," Anna continued.

A bible and three books were next in the box of goodies. Strips of soft cotton batting were wrapped around the next item to appear.

"This will be the inside of our quilt," Anna explained.

Slowly and carefully she unwound the layers. The valued object was soon revealed when a beautifully polished mahogany guitar appeared. Anna plucked the pick from the neck of the guitar and started strumming. She sang quietly in a soft sweet voice.

"We'll have lots of fun singing. I know many songs and brought a song book with me."

The girls nodded their heads, their wide eyes bright and sparkling.

Anna laid the instrument down. She reached deep into the trunk for the final few items. Several lace handkerchiefs were wound around two brooches, three necklaces, earrings, hair combs and pins. Tucked into the corner and wrapped in a red woollen scarf were a brush, hand mirror and comb. Made of ivory there was a trailing rose design imbedded on the handles. The opposite corner produced six balls of yarn. Brightly colored ribbons of every hue were wound around each ball: green, red, blue, yellow, purple and white — a satin rainbow of ribbons.

Chapter 8

Mrs. Bailey made several trips to the little house. She taught Anna about the fine art of cooking. Katy's garden produced many vegetables. Peas, beans, carrots and beets were canned for winter eating. Potatoes, turnips, onions and carrots were dug and stored in a root cellar for future use. Katy and Sarah couldn't wait to get home from school and sample the latest baking.

Mr. Bailey and Tommy arrived one day. They loaded one of the pigs into the wagon. It was taken to the Bailey farm and butchered. After it was cut up and cured, half would be returned for the family to use. The Bailey's would use the rest.

One sunny day in mid-September heralded the arrival of the threshing crew. Tommy came over early and helped Katy set boards across log stumps to form a long table and benches. Then they left to go and help the group of men working out in the field.

The little kitchen was a beehive of activity. Mrs. Bailey came over and supervised Anna and Sarah. Loaves of freshly baked bread and fruit pies were lined up on the stove. Potatoes, carrots, turnips and tomatoes from Katy's garden were added to the browned pork.

"Let's make some dumplings to add to the stew," Mrs. Bailey said just minutes before the men were due to arrive.

"See, like this: flour, water and baking powder stirred together, and then dropped into the simmering pot on the stove. These lumps of dough will firm up and make the stew even better. They will taste like a soft biscuit." Ma's special pickles were added to the hearty meal.

The crew arrived promptly at 12 noon. Gruff voices from the tired men soon became quiet as they dug into full dishes of wholesome food. The girls were kept busy filling dishes and serving mugs of strong black coffee. Anna's light voice chattered happily as she passed out second pieces of pie to the weary workers. They nodded their thanks and hurried out to continue with the harvesting.

~~~~~~

As fall settled in, the days got shorter. Leaves on the trees and shrubs turned vibrant shades of gold and red. Two windy days in a row released the few trees of their colorful burden. The resulting leafy carpet soon turned into a brown crunchy mass and drifted away in the autumn breeze.

Katy rode Sam and Sarah rode Little Red to school every day. Katy thought school was okay but was always excited to get home and work outdoors.

"Katy, don't you get tired doing the chores all alone?" a concerned Anna asked her one day.

"I really like working with the animals. They need to be looked after," Katy shrugged matter of factly.

One evening after supper, Katy was heading out the door to tend to the chores.

"I thought maybe I could start teaching you girls about sewing," Anna said.

"That might be a good idea, but I don't think I'd be much good at it," Katy replied. "I guess I should learn, though."

Anna carefully cut a square of material for each of the girls.

"I thought we could each work on a patch. You can do your own design on your square. Just draw something easy with a pencil and then stitch around it," Anna instructed. "When we've finished enough we'll sew them together. Maybe we can make a new quilt for your Pa when he comes home."

The girls agreed this would be a good idea. Threading the needle was the first major step and not nearly as easy as it looked.

"Wet the end of the thread on your tongue," Anna advised. "Then it will slide easier into the eye of the needle."

After much frustration the needles were finally all loaded. Anna was helping Rebecca because she was still very young.

"Now it's time to knot the thread," Anna announced.

She could rub the double thread through her thumb and finger and miraculously in a flash it was a knot. Try as they might, the girls could not master this part. Finally they simply tied one knot on top of another. The result was the same.

"Now poke the needle through the material, make a very small stitch and bring it back up," Anna suggested. This, too, was not as simple as it sounded. Two hours and only a half dozen stitches later, Katy put her craft down.

"Guess we'd better be going to bed now. I think it will take years to get a quilt made," she said disgustedly.

"Don't worry; you'll get faster with practice," Anna said patiently. "We'll work on it a little at a time and have it ready in the spring."

Chapter 9

Miss Holmes rode her horse out to the farm most Fridays after school. She would stay over until Sunday and go into church with the girls. The little house was full of giggles and fun when they all got together. Anna tried some of her new cooking skills on everyone. One time she forgot to put yeast in the bread dough. The result resembled a hard, flat rock.

"I've got an idea," Katy laughed. "Let's take it outside and see who can throw it the furthest."

After the dishes and chores were done, Anna brought her guitar out and started strumming. They spent the evening singing old songs and new ones they were learning.

"Here, Katy, see if you can play," Anna offered one evening.

"I'd really like to play," Katy replied shyly. "Do you think I could learn?"

Anna taught her how to strum a few notes. After that every opportunity she had Katy would practice. Soon she was playing chords on her own.

Mrs. Bailey was over visiting with the girls one day in late October.

"You know, Anna, much as I love having the little fellow, I think maybe it's time for Jacob to return to his real family. You think you can handle that?" Mrs. Bailey inquired.

"Yes, Emma, I think you're probably right. I was thinking about that the other day. Jacob should be living with us now."

"Why don't you and your family come for supper next Saturday and we'll keep him here?" Anna suggested.

Early Friday morning Katy headed out to do chores.

"Katy, could you get me a couple of chickens for us to do up for supper with the Bailey's tomorrow?" Anna inquired.

Katy nodded. "I'll do it tonight."

Riding Sam home after school, Katy's stomach suddenly fluttered when she thought about the chickens. She had watched Pa butcher them, but never done it herself.

Supper finished, Katy headed out to the chicken coop. With her heart in her throat she grabbed one innocent bird by the legs and walked to the chopping block outside the door. The chicken struggled and flapped its wings in protest. Katy laid the chicken on the stump, lifted the axe, closed her eyes and chopped. A huge squawk and blood squirted everywhere. Katy released the chicken's legs and the poor headless creature circled crazily around the yard before falling over. The second chicken was a little easier. She held onto the legs until the chicken was completely lifeless. Katy stripped the feathers off the birds and pulled the innards out.

The next day, a cool, crisp Saturday afternoon, the Bailey family arrived in their wagon. Wonderful scents greeted them as they approached the house. Katy and Anna had laid planks over stumps in the living room to have a table big enough to feed everyone.

"You girls should be real proud," Emma Bailey said, obviously enjoying the feast before her. Mashed potatoes, carrots, peas, roast chicken with dressing and lumpy gravy were set out on the table.

"This stuffing is really good. There seems to be a different flavor in it." Emma said appreciatively.

"As you know, I never cooked at home," Anna replied. "I always remember my Grandma's secret ingredient in her famous dressing was cinnamon, so I tried it. I need to work on my gravy making, though."

A huge bowl of apple crisp, still steaming from the oven, completed the meal.

Tommy helped Katy with chores as the others cleaned up from supper. Anna brought out her guitar. Mr. Bailey disappeared for a minute. He returned with a gunny sack wrapped around something. He laid it in front of Katy.

"This is for you to use for a while," he said gruffly.

Startled, Katy pulled the burlap off and looked down in surprise. Before her lay an old guitar.

"Where did this come from?" she asked softly.

"Belonged to my Grandpa. Hasn't been used for a long time. Figured maybe you would like it."

"Oh, thank you, Mr. Bailey. I will take very good care of it." She gently lifted the instrument and lovingly caressed the smooth surface. Katy laid it across her lap and plucked at each of the strings. Though slightly out of key, it sounded so sweet to her ears. Anna strummed and Katy chorded. Everyone joined in singing the old favorite songs. Even Jacob clapped his chubby little hands happily.

"We have to go home now," Mrs. Bailey announced. "Time to do chores. I will surely miss this little boy, but he should be living with his own family."

With tears in her eyes she kissed Jacob goodbye.

"We'll see all of you often. Call on us if you need anything."

~~~~~~~

By late November the days were much shorter. Katy had to break a thin layer of ice off the water trough each morning. Nobody delayed on their trips to the outhouse. The tall grass and shrubs by the barn were coated in a shimmery frosting. Katy's breath produced small puffs of smoke and when Buster ran up to greet her, he displayed a frothy white beard. Katy wore her heavy coat and the bright red mittens and hat Ma had knit for her last year.

Chapter 10

One Friday evening Miss Holmes came to spend the weekend with the family.

"Anna, now that you know how to drive the horse and wagon, why don't you go and visit Mrs. Bailey tomorrow?" she suggested. "You need to get out a little. I thought Katy, Sarah and I could start practicing for the Christmas concert. Maybe Tommy and Matt could come over and practice too."

Two Saturdays earlier the little family had gone into town to purchase supplies for the winter. Anna had a lesson on driving the team of horses. Katy sat beside her and guided her along the way. Pa left money he made at the logging camp in his account at the store. The girls picked up some dry goods: flour, sugar, salt and a few other necessities.

Anna drove the team and wagon home afterwards. Except for a few shaky starts she was able to guide them all the way home without any problems.

Early Saturday morning Anna set out for the Bailey place. Rebecca and Jacob were bundled in blankets in the back of the wagon. A pile of loose hay and a sack of things Anna was taking with her, provided protection and warmth for the two small children. Anna snapped the reins and they set off at a fast clip over the frost covered prairie. Tommy and Matt Bailey rode their horses over so they could practice with the girls.

The children spent the morning making Christmas decorations. They formed strips of catalogue pages into long chains to be strung across the room at the school house. After dinner at noon, Katy brought out her guitar. They sang Christmas songs. Katy and Sarah sang duets in soft sweet voices. Finally after some encouragement the two boys shyly joined in on a few of the popular carols. This routine continued for the next few weeks, usually on Saturday mornings.

Anna and Emma were busy preparing Christmas baking over at the Bailey place. The Bailey's had invited everyone for Christmas dinner at their home. Mr. Bailey had a big turkey he was growing to be the main attraction on the dinner table. Katy was so glad she didn't have to worry about capturing and preparing the big bird.

During the long evenings in December Anna, Katy, Sarah and Rebecca sat in the light of the coal oil lamp and sewed their pieces of material. They were getting better at it and had a pile of about twenty squares completed. Even Rebecca, with Anna's help, stitched little x's on her patches, She said they were kisses. The other girls formed stars, flowers and hearts on their squares.

One cold Friday in December, Katy, bundled in a warm coat, ran out to do her chores. Anna was a little sad because they wouldn't have a tree to decorate for Christmas. There were no fir trees, few trees of any sort around. Katy had an idea. She raced out behind the barn and there it was, huddled against the fence, a huge Russian thistle about 3 ½ feet tall. A weed, it was round with spiny branches and was quite prickly. Katy reached low down with her mittened hands and gave a mighty heave. She grunted and struggled until finally the roots broke free. Katy landed on her bottom with the big prickly bush in her hands. She lugged the thistle into the barn. She placed the little tree into a pail half full of dirt and dragged the whole thing to the house.

"Anna, come here!" she shouted. "I want to show you something."

Anna hurried over. "What have you got there, Katy?" Curiosity was etched on her face.

"I thought if we shaped this a little, it would make a Christmas tree," Katy explained slowly.

"What a good idea. Let's go do it right now." Anna clapped her hands enthusiastically. "Thank you for doing this for us."

The Russian thistle was cut into a rough tree shape. Paper chains were looped around it. The pail was decorated and the whole thing set up on the mantle. The Bailey family and Miss Holmes were visiting. Everyone agreed this was the most beautiful tree ever.

"I have an idea. Let's do something fun to celebrate," Anna announced happily. "I'm going to cook up some taffy. I used to make it at home."

She poured sugar, molasses and water into a pot on the stove. After the concoction boiled and thickened a bit it was tested. A few drops of the syrup were dropped into a cup of cold water to see if they formed into hard balls. When this occurred, it was time to pour it into a pan and cool it for a while.

"Each of you will get a piece of this candy which is called taffy. Two of you work together, each pulling an end. Stretch it out a few times between you. When it turns a light yellow color, you can form it into a long twisted rope. Cut it into smaller pieces and let it harden. Then you will have some delicious candy to eat.

Matt and Rebecca, Katy and Tommy, Sarah and Miss Holmes, and Anna and Mrs. Bailey paired up. Mr. Bailey held Jacob on his knee and watched the fun. Except for Rebecca getting a piece of taffy caught in her hair, everything went smoothly. They all agreed the sweet treat was yummy.

~~~~~~~

On the final Saturday before the Christmas concert, both families and Miss Holmes met at the little farm house. Before dinner, the 12 students of different ages had been practicing their play at school. Costumes were fashioned out of towels and crepe paper.

The two families finished dinner.

"I have a surprise everyone," the bubbly Anna announced.

"Let's make some popcorn and we'll string it for decorations."

The girls giggled. They had done this before. It meant threading needles to pierce through the popcorn. They started at once.

Anna disappeared to her bedroom for a few minutes. She returned with a pile of colorful material in her arms.

"I thought you needed some new dresses for the Christmas concert," she said excitedly. "I used some of your ma's old dresses and added lace I brought with me."

"Those Saturdays over at my house," Mrs. Bailey explained. "Anna's been sewing on my old machine. She wanted to surprise you."

The girls, wide eyes shining, each grabbed a garment.

"Try them on," Anna encouraged. Katy, Sarah and Rebecca paraded around in their new finery. Twirling round and round the full skirts billowed out around them.

"They are so beautiful, thank you, thank you, thank you, Anna," the three girls echoed happily.

The Bailey family snug in their winter coats, climbed into the wagon.

"See you next Friday at the school concert," Mrs. Bailey boomed heartily as the horses trotted into the inky darkness.

Chapter 11

Katy woke up early on Friday morning. She lay still beneath the warm covers for a minute. A tickle of excitement in her stomach reminded her this was the big day. She rolled out of bed and quickly slipped into her warm clothes. It was pitch dark outside as she closed the door quietly behind her. Katy wanted to get chores done early today. After milking Bessie and Bossy, she slapped them on the rump. The two cows moved sluggishly out the barn door. They headed toward the pasture mooing their disapproval. Five kittens from Misty's latest litter came running up to her purring loudly. They caught the scent of the fresh milk. Katy spilt a little milk into a saucer in the corner. The kittens tumbled over each other in their haste to slurp up the treat.

"You greedy little things," Katy chuckled.

As she left the barn, a brilliant streak of pink was peeking through the light clouds to the east. Katy took the pail of warm milk and poured it into the separator. She cranked the handle to set the bowls on the machine revolving. The cream would drain into the smaller container and the milk into the larger one. Later some cream would be churned until it turned into butter. The milk products were stored in containers set in a large pail. The pail had a rope attached to the handle. It was lowered into the well to keep cool.

Katy threw some grain out for the chickens that were rooting around in the dry grass. She collected eggs and poured a mixture of mash into the trough for the pigs.

~~~~~~~

Katy and Sarah riding Sam and little Red galloped into their yard early Friday afternoon after school. Miss Holmes had let the kids go home early on Friday so they could get ready for the concert later in the evening.

After chores and supper the girls put on their new dresses. Anna combed their long hair until it shone. Each of the girls had a ribbon and bow matching her dress color woven into her hair. Everyone loaded into the wagon. Katy was driving the team. Anna sat with a warmly wrapped Jacob on her knee in the passenger seat. The two younger girls were tucked between the straw and wrapped in cozy blankets. Large stones had been heated by the stove. Covered with burlap they kept the feet toasty warm. Katy had attached a string of bells on the harness. She snapped the reins and urged the horses on. The air was crisp and puffs of steam blew from the noses of the snorting horses. The bells jingled merrily and the happy group joined in singing Jingle Bells.

Excitement was crackling in the air when they arrived at the school yard. This was the big event of the winter and everyone looked forward to it.

Inside the classroom, a bed sheet was hung over a rope to conceal the stage. Wooden benches were set up in rows for the audience. After people were seated, the curtain was slowly pulled back. A sudden hush filled the room. Two of the smallest children spoke in timid voices. Guided by Miss Holmes from the sidelines, they nervously welcomed everyone. The children had various parts as they performed the story of the first Christmas. The curtain closed and the audience clapped and stomped their feet.

The curtain opened again and the children were all gathered around Katy. She started strumming her guitar. Soon everyone whether they could sing or not, joined in various renditions of the old Christmas favorites.

Suddenly bells started jingling. In bounced jolly old Santa Claus.

"HO, HO, HO, MERRY CHRISTMAS BOYS AND GIRLS," he boomed. Out of his sack came some treats. A pencil with an eraser on the end was handed to each child. Then he produced a goody bag with a few peanuts, an orange and several candies in it.

The men moved the benches to the side of the room. Oscar jumped onto the stage with his accordion. Old Joe followed with his fiddle.

"Grab yer partners for a square dance," he hollered. Red-faced boys, with some encouragement from their parents asked girls to dance. The giggling girls shyly accepted the awkward invitations. A blushing Tommy asked Katy to be his partner. Soon the little room was a buzzing swarm of dancers. The women and girls swirled around in their colorful new dresses, feeling very special. Small children moved in and out among the dancers. Men wore new bib overalls, a well-worn suit or whatever they had. It didn't really matter. No one had much money. They knew how to make do with what they had.

The dancing continued for about two hours. Having worked up an appetite everyone ate the sandwiches and sweets the ladies had brought. Slowly they started gathering their belongings, including small children and babies who were sound asleep on blankets laid out in the coat room. The wagons rolled out of the school yard amid laughter and greetings of "Merry Christmas."

A full moon shining on the light coating of sparkling frost on the ground provided a bright light for the journey home.

Chapter 12

It was Christmas Eve and Saturday night baths were completed.

"Are you going to hang your stockings up?" Anna inquired.

"I didn't think we would do it this year," Katy answered slowly. "Ma and Pa aren't here."

I think you should anyway," Anna said as she helped Rebecca find a stocking. Katy and Sarah ran to their room and each returned with long stockings.

"I brought a spare one of mine for Jacob," Katy chuckled. "His are way too small to hold anything."

Katy woke up early. She stoked the stove and dressed warmly. She ran quietly outside into the cool, crisp morning and hurried with her chores. When she returned to the house, everyone was up and dressed. The little kitchen was warm. Katy noticed the sock on the floor by the small Christmas tree was bulging slightly

"Girls you better go check to see if Santa came," a smiling Anna suggested.

The girls took turns emptying their socks. Each one found a pretty lace handkerchief with her own initial embroidered on it. A bright hair ribbon, mitts and a scarf tumbled out. A stick of peppermint candy and an orange were in the toe of the sock.

"Look," Katy pointed to the floor. "Even Jacob got a little pair of mittens. He'll have fun with that ball, too." Jacob was more interested in sucking on the ball than playing with it.

"We're all so lucky," Sarah whispered softly.

"We are, but I feel bad you didn't get anything, Anna," Katy added sadly.

"But I did," Anna laughed. "Remember you made that beautiful little tree for us and I have a family now. That is my very special Christmas gift. In fact I think it's the best one I've ever had."

"I'm starving, let's eat," she continued. "Sarah helped me make scrambled eggs and pancakes."

After breakfast everyone piled into the wagon for the trek to the Bailey house. Anna took along two mincemeat pies she had baked for the dinner. She packed a small gift she was taking for Mrs. Bailey.

Tommy and Matt ran outside as soon as the jangling bells on the wagon announced their arrival. Happy greetings of Merry Christmas echoed in the frosty air. Mrs. Bailey, cheerful and excited, hugged everyone. The two boys and Katy took the horses to the barn.

"Here, Emma, this is a little something I made for you," Anna said as she handed her the roll of material. Mrs. Bailey was trembling as she slowly unfurled the length of red silk.

Tiny stitches marched around the edge of the table runner. A little Christmas tree was embroidered in green on each end. Small initials, E.B. were stitched in one corner.

"This is so beautiful," Mrs. Bailey sighed shakily. "I never get presents." A tear rolled down her cheek as she hugged Anna.

"I was happy to do something for you, Emma. You've been a good friend and you've helped me so much. I can never repay you enough."

"Come on kids," Mr. Bailey said. "Let's go down to the pond. It's frozen over now and you can slide on it, if you want. We'll let the women get supper ready."

The children bundled up and went outside for some fresh air and exercise.

When they returned awhile later, the wonderful aroma of turkey filled the air. The large table was full of delicious things: creamy mashed potatoes, carrots and peas, a bowl of canned tomatoes, fresh buns and butter, gravy and dill pickles. The huge turkey, browned to perfection, sat on a platter in front of Mr. Bailey's spot at the head of the table. After saying grace, he carved the turkey and passed it around. Mincemeat pie and shortbread completed the Christmas feast.

"Guess we'll have to be heading home soon, Katy announced. "Still have to do chores when I get home."

Katy went out to the barn to help Tommy and Matt do their chores. They harnessed the horses for the return trip home.

Meanwhile Sarah, Anna and Emma cleared up after the big meal. Mr. Bailey and Rebecca amused Jacob with some blocks Mr. Bailey had carved out of pieces of wood.

Thank you, Mr. and Mrs. Bailey," Katy said as she walked out the door. We had a very happy Christmas with all of you. The rest of the group shouted thank yous and good byes as they climbed aboard the wagon for the trip home.

Chapter 13

The weather remained cool and crisp for another two weeks. One Saturday in mid-January heavy white clouds moved across the sky. Soon large flakes of snow started falling slowly and softly. Before long the ground was totally covered in a pillowy white blanket. Katy, Sarah and Rebbeca quickly dressed in their warm winter clothes and ran outside. Anna finally followed after dressing a squirming Jacob in a bulky snowsuit.

"Look," Rebecca squealed. Where'd the snow go?" She was running around with her mouth wide open. Her pink tongue was sticking out of her mouth.

"Silly girl," Sarah chuckled. "Your warm tongue melts the snow as soon as it lands."

"C'mon girls," Katy instructed. She quickly hopped over to a pile of pure white fluff. "Lay down flat on your back beside me." The girls obeyed. "Now flap your arms up and down. Move your legs back and forth sideways. She demonstrated as she talked. Jump up now." The three girls skipped forward and turned around.

"See the angels we made in the snow? They look like they are dancing, holding hands."

Katy took off running toward the barn. She returned pulling a sled with a shaggy piece of rope attached to it. There was a wooden box fastened to the sleigh.

"Let's put Jacob in and give him rides." A big quilt tucked in secured Jacob and kept him warm as well. The girls took turns pulling Jacob, then Rebecca, around the yard. Buster ran in frantic circles around everyone. Sounds of laughter and the occasional dog bark echoed across the open prairie.

"I'd better go and get the big sleigh ready for the horses to pull us to church tomorrow," Katy announced. "Remember the Bailey's are coming over after church."

"Coming for my birfday party." Rebecca giggled excitedly.

"We'd better go inside and get the cake finished for tomorrow," Anna said. She headed to the house carrying a red-cheeked Jacob.

"Don't forget we're celebrating Matt's birthday, too," Anna reminded the little girl.

The snow continued all night. Katy pushed with all her might to get the door open in the morning when she went out to do chores. It was still dark outside. Katy plodded through the snow to the barn. She grabbed the shovel and made a path from the house to the barn and the outhouse beside it. By the time chores were finished and Katy emerged from the barn, the snow had stopped. Streaks of orange stretched across the eastern sky as the sun struggled to make an appearance. Bessy and Bossy slowly shuffled out to pasture. As usual, they softly mooed their annoyance.

Katy harnessed the horses to the sleigh. After breakfast the little group tumbled into the straw covered cutter. Katy picked up the reins and encouraged the horses on. They were soon trotting at a brisk pace across the snow-covered prairie. The skis on the sled hummed as they skimmed over the perfect white snow.

After church the Bailey's and Miss Holmes drove their team out to the farm. They ate an early afternoon dinner. Everyone except Rebecca and Jacob played cards. Rebecca was busy crooning to her new baby. Mrs. Bailey and Anna had given her a little doll they had fashioned out of wool. Buttons were stitched on the face to form eyes, nose and mouth. A piece of fabric was stitched into a dress for the doll. Rebecca wrapped her doll in scraps of material. She gently laid her baby in a cardboard box bed. Jacob, tired from the busy day, was napping in the corner.

"Katy, Tommy, we should go out and chop some of those logs up," Mr. Bailey suggested. The trio headed to the big pile of wood stacked against the barn.

"You need to be sure and have lots of kindling in the cold weather," Mr. Bailey advised. "Never know when you could be snowed in."

Logs had been sawed into pieces the length of a man's arm. Tommy helped his dad tug one of the huge logs onto a flat end. Mr. Bailey picked up the axe. He arced it back over his shoulder. With a mighty heave and a grunt, he swung downward. The razor sharp edge of the axe cut the log cleanly in half.

"I'll do a few more logs, and then you two can take turns cutting them smaller for the stove," the older man instructed. "Be real careful you don't cut your foot. That axe is very sharp."

~~~~~~~

February 14th was on a Friday. The night before Anna, Katy, Sarah and Rebecca drew hearts and designs on paper. They colored them red and folded them up. Katy and Sarah were taking theirs to school. Miss Holmes was having a little party. The girls took heart shaped cookies they had helped bake.

"You got lots of Valentines, Katy," Sarah teased. "Even Tommy gave you one."

"So what," Katy countered. "I notice you got one from Matt."

Both girls laughed as they coaxed their horses into a gallop for the ride home. There was still quite a bit of snow on the ground, but not enough to slow the horses down.

Chapter 14

Early one Tuesday afternoon the beginning of March, the kids were in the little schoolhouse working on spelling. Miss Holmes had been keeping a watchful eye on the sky outside the window. By two o'clock the clouds had turned very dark and heavy, hanging low in a threatening sky.

"Class, I think you'd better get your outdoor clothes on and hurry home," she said seriously. "Don't dawdle, looks like a storm might be coming."

Katy and Sarah quickly struggled into their coats, boots and hats. They had heavy socks on, which they pulled up high. Miss Holmes wrapped a long woollen scarf around each girl's head and face, leaving only their eyes exposed. The two sisters ran out the door, over to the hitching post and untied their horses. A vicious wind was churning the snow into whipped cream piles. Large flakes of snow were falling from the sky all but obliterating the horizon.

"I'll ride ahead and lead the way, Sarah. You can follow close behind." The words blew from Katy's mouth into the frozen air. The girls jumped on Sam and Little Red They picked up the reins and prodded the horses in the ribs. Slowly the animals, with heads lowered, plodded forward into the blustery white landscape. The girls, riding bareback travelled for about twenty minutes before the blizzard hit with all its fury. Snow swirled round and round. The trail was piled high with soft snow. Tall rounded banks were forming over the weeds and grass at the side of the trail.

When she turned to check behind her, Katy could barely see Sarah's bright red scarf whipping furiously in the wind.

"Hang on, Sarah," she shouted, but her words were lost as soon as she uttered them. Sam plunged forward into a snow bank. Katy twisted around again just in time to see Little Red stumble. Sarah pitched sideways and fell face first into the deep snow. Katy pulled back on the reins to stop Sam. She slid off the big horse. Katy bounded awkwardly toward her sister. The tumble spooked Little Red who took off with her lines dragging beside her.

"Sarah, Sarah, are you okay?" Katy puffed as she knelt into the snow beside her sister.

"I-I d-don't know," a shivering Sarah stammered.

"You have to get up," Katy begged as she struggled to pull her sister to her feet.

"I c-can't."

"You have to move, Sarah, or you'll freeze to death," Katy commanded sharply. "C'mon now, I'll push you onto Sam's back. You'll have to try and help me."

She put her arm around her sister, half dragging her to the patiently waiting horse. With a huge shove from behind, Sarah finally settled on Sam's back. She clung to Sam's frosty mane. Katy climbed on back behind her sister. She wrapped her arm around Sarah's waist. Katy picked up the reins, but soon realized she had no idea where she was. The blizzard had created a total white out. Katy coaxed the big horse on. Sam took a few awkward steps, paused, and then stopped completely. He refused to move. Sarah was trembling and sobbing.

"Katy, I'm s-so c-cold," she stuttered, the words muffled as they escaped through her scarf.

"You have to stay awake, Sarah, move your hands and feet as much as you can. I remember Pa telling us one time if you let your horse go on its own, it'll take you home. Horses have an inner sense to return to where they are fed. Let's give it a try."

"Please, God, help us to get home safely." Katy sent a silent prayer heavenward.

The two girls huddled low on Sam's back. Katy released her hold on the reins. She wrapped her arms around Sarah's waist. Sarah was still gripping Sam's mane in her cold stiffened hands. Slowly Sam raised one hoof, then another. Soon he was striding awkwardly through the heavy snow. Katy continued talking into Sarah's ear attempting to keep the younger girl awake. It seemed they rode a very long way, the snow piling high on horse and riders. Finally Sam stopped. Katy raised her head and peeked through her frost crusted eyelashes. She saw the faint outline of the barn in front of them.

"Sam, Sam," she sobbed. You did it! You brought us home." The white shadow of Little Red stood near the steps. She nickered a greeting to Sam.

"Sarah, c'mon let's go inside and get warm." No response.

"I-I can't m-move," Sarah finally mumbled faintly.

Katy pushed her sister and she rolled off the big horse's back. She landed with a thud in a deep pile of snow. Katy slid down stiffly. She put her arm around her sister's limp form and lifted the motionless girl. She slowly dragged her up the porch steps. Katy banged on the door. Anna appeared in the doorway. She saw the two half frozen figures in front of her.

"I'm so glad you finally got home. I've been so worried." Tears streamed down Anna's cheeks as she pulled the girls over close to the stove. She removed the stiff clothing from Katy and Sarah. She rubbed their hands and feet to get the blood circulating. Anna wrapped blankets around the girls.

"I'll make some hot cocoa. It'll warm you up inside, too."

After she finished the hot drink, Katy went to the coat hooks by the door.

"Anna I'm going to wear your dry coat outside. I have to get Sam warmed up and fed. You know he saved our lives today."

Anna smiled as she nodded in agreement.

~~~~~~~

With a mighty push, Katy got the door open. She fought her way through the blinding snowstorm. She pulled Sam by the halter toward the barn.

Poor Sam had snow embedded in his fur. Icicles hung from his nostrils and his eyelashes were etched in frost. Small puffs of steam blowing through his nose created a hazy cloud around his head. Katy threw a blanket on his back. She gave him fresh hay.

"Here, boy, a special treat for you." Katy shoved a pail of oats under Sam's nose. "Thank you for getting us home safely today." She patted the horse affectionately.

Katy fed Little Red and the rest of the animals. They were all safely in the shelter now. Even the chickens were content to stay indoors.

On her way back to the house, Katy tied one end of a long rope to the barn door. She pulled the heavy cable along with her and tied the other end on the house door. Pa had told her about this one time. Whenever Katy had to go out in the blizzard, she would have the rope to direct her. She would not lose her way.

The little house remained snowbound for the next two days. The wind blew fiercely and constantly. Snow piled in deep drifts against the house and barn. Katy would shovel snow outside the door to clear a path each time she left the house. Her rope lifeline guided her as she did the chores.

Katy made many trips outside to bring in wood to stoke the stove. She was grateful for Mr. Bailey's earlier instructions to have plenty of wood chopped and ready. Katy brought pails of snow to heat on the stove so they would have water to use. The reservoir on the far side of the stove was always filled with warm water.

Anna was frowning when Katy stomped her way into the house.

"I'm worried about your sister. She's very hot and has a bad cough."

Later that evening Sarah was much worse. Her chest appeared to be very congested. Her breathing was shallow. Sarah was trembling as though cold, but was burning up with a fever.

"I remember one time when I was little I had a chest cold. I could hardly breathe," Katy explained. "Ma made me something called a mustard plaster. I think it was made of flour, mustard and warm water. It was mixed together and made into a thick paste. Then it was spread on a towel and wrapped like a package."

"Let's try it." Anna was already searching for the ingredients. She laid the towel wrapped mustard plaster on Sarah's chest. The smell of it was strong and not very nice.

Anna and Katy took turns sitting with Sarah. They warmed the plaster when it cooled down. Finally in the early morning hours, Anna laid her cool hand on Sarah's forehead.

"I need a drink," Sarah moaned softly.

"The fever has broken," a relieved Anna whispered as she rushed over to get a cup of water.

Chapter 15

The next morning when Katy woke up, she lay still for a minute. Something was different. It was totally quiet. No wind was whistling around the corners of the little house.

Katy got up quickly and bundled into her warm clothing. She pushed with all her strength against the door. Suddenly, it gave way and the door slowly creaked open. Katy ploughed her way to the barn. She realized it had warmed up considerably. When Katy opened the barn door, Buster rushed out. He was happy to be released from his confinement of the last few days.

~~~~~~~

Later in the morning, Buster let out a couple of sharp barks. Someone pounded insistently on the door. Anna rushed over. Mr. Bailey and Tommy stamped the snow off their boots as they entered the kitchen.

"Just came over to see if you all are okay." Mr. Bailey said as he peeled off his mitts. "Sure was a bad storm we had."

"Sam got the girls home from school safely. Katy knew what to do." Anna replied seriously. "Sarah was very sick, but her temperature finally went down. She's getting better. Katy looked after the chores and we stayed warm. We were very lucky."

"Poor old Clem got caught in the blizzard coming home from town," Mr. Bailey explained sadly. "Got confused and ended up lost in the white-out. Found him frozen stiff in his pasture yesterday."

"Tommy and I will help you clear a path to the barn, Katy," Mr. Bailey said as he headed outside.

The trio went out into the sunny crisp day. They shovelled paths to the various outbuildings to make it easier to get around. When they were finished, Anna served them big bowls of freshly made hot soup with warm biscuits.

"Emma said to come over on the weekend, if you're able." Mr. Bailey said as he mounted his horse. "I'm thinking she's pretty lonely after the storm."

"We'll be happy to come over if we can," Anna smiled. "We sure could use a change of scene too."

Chapter 16

It was mid-April and most of the snow had melted. Late evenings and early mornings the haunting chorus of coyotes howling echoed across the prairie. Buster would soon join in with his deep-throated yowl, adding to the commotion.

Evenings after supper and chores, the girls continued working on their patches. They were almost finished. The bright assortment was laid out on the floor in a pattern. Anna would stitch them together to make the quilt.

May arrived in sunny, bright splendor. Buds were forming on the trees. Crocuses pushed small purple heads through the dry, weed-infested field. Tinges of new green brightened the dull brown grass in the pasture. A few birds were heralding the slow arrival of spring.

On a Saturday in early May after chores, Katy bounced into the house.

"Anna, I'm going to dig up some dirt close to the house. Then we can plant those seeds you brought with you."

"Oh, thank you," Anna replied cheerfully. "I can hardly wait to have some flowers again."

Rebecca ran toward the house, hands behind her back.

"What have you got there, dear?" a smiling Anna asked.

"These are for you," Rachel giggled as she presented a bunch of slightly crushed velvety crocuses to Anna.

Mr. Bailey and Tommy dropped by in the afternoon.

"Thought we'd let you know, a crew of neighbors will be by next week. Help put the crop in." Mr. Bailey drawled. "Emma said she'll come and help cook."

The neighboring men and machinery arrived on Wednesday morning. They ploughed the fields, and then seeded them. Katy stayed home from school and helped where she was needed. Although not strong enough for some tasks, she was very determined. She was constantly busy doing whatever she could out in the field.

The women and girls prepared fried chicken, potato salad and biscuits for the hungry workers. The food would be washed down with lemonade or coffee. Cake completed the meal.

Katy managed to plough the garden patch herself. Then she planted row upon row of potatoes, turnips, carrots and beets. Several rows of peas, beans, a few tomatoes and pumpkins completed her vegetable plot.

Anna wandered outside carrying a squirming Jacob.

"Katy, I can't believe you did this all by yourself," she exclaimed. She watched the young girl with grimy smudges on her face as she patted dirt over the seeds.

"I really enjoy gardening," Katy replied as she brushed the hair out of her eyes. Another streak of dust clung to her forehead. "It's a miracle how a tiny seed can grow into something to eat."

A big celebration was being planned for early June. It was a little late for Jacob's first birthday, Sarah's 10th and Katy's 14th. The weather was warm. The family was happy to have survived a whole year without Ma and Pa being there.

Chapter 17

Neighbors started arriving around one o'clock on Sunday after church. The ladies brought their own specialty food to share. Various delights set out on the plank tables presented a feast. Huge jugs of lemonade and coffee sat on a table loaded with sweet dessert treats.

Families spread blankets on the ground to sit on. Small children ran around playing tag. Teenagers nervously teased each other, blushing when they were noticed. The ladies were admiring the beautiful handiwork on the special quilt. It was hung proudly with pins on the clothesline for all to see. Some stitches weren't perfect, but it was truly a work of art with a story attached to it. Men stood in clusters discussing weather and crops.

"Let's have a game of ball," someone yelled. Older children and teenagers and people of all ages and sizes lined up to choose teams. The others watched and cheered their team on.

A stream of dust was billowing across the prairie toward the house. Soon a rider on horseback was in sight.

"Pa! Pa's home!" Katy screamed as she raced from her position on second base to the approaching horseman. Sarah and Rebecca followed her waving their arms wildly. The large bay mare stopped suddenly in a swirl of grit and Pa leaped out of the saddle with arms outstretched. Katy, Sarah and Rebecca all jumped on him nearly knocking him over.

"Pa, Papa, we're so glad you're home," they sang out excitedly.

"I'm very happy to see you, too," Pa replied in a choked voice. "You all have grown."

Anna sauntered over with Jacob on her hip.

"Hello, I'm Anna," she said. Her bright red pony tail bounced jauntily and her brilliant green eyes sparkled happily.

"I'm pleased to meet you, ma'am," Pa said as he tipped his hat to her. Taking her small hand into his big one, he gently squeezed. "I want to thank you for caring for my family."

"You are most welcome, Mr. Robertson. "It was my pleasure and we had lots of fun as well."

"I'd like you to call me Charlie," Pa said.

"Now, Charlie, I'd like you to meet your son Jacob," Anna said. She tried to pry the little guy's arms from around her neck, but he wouldn't let go. Jacob took one look at the big rugged looking man in a black cowboy hat. He buried his face against Anna's shoulder and clung to her.

"Guess it'll take him a little time to get used to you," Anna smiled.

The group of neighbours crowded around Pa. "Welcome back, good to have you home," they chorused taking turns shaking his hand.

"Come on, girls, grab your guitars," Oscar announced suddenly. He and Joe took their instruments out. "This is a real celebration now your Pa's home."

Anna handed Jacob to Sarah to look after. Stomping his foot, Oscar squeezed the music box. Joe stroked the bow across the strings on his fiddle. Katy and Anna strummed on their guitars. Soon the little band had a lively tune going. Small children, bigger kids, adults alike, clapped and moved in rhythm to the music.

"Grab your partners for a square dance," Oscar bellowed.

Pa approached Anna. "Would you honor me with a dance?" Anna laid her guitar down. "Yes, I would like that."

Pa looked over at Katy. "I'm real proud of you, Katy girl, playing that guitar."

~~~~~~~

Bright streaks of pink across the western sky announced the end of another day. Happy folks helped clean up after the party. They gathered their families and belongings. Piling into waiting wagons, they waved vigorously. Shouts of thank you and good bye resounded across the expanse. Pa went into the little house with his family.

"It's good to be home," he announced. "I'm hoping you're able to stay on, Anna. When I got off the stage in town, I dropped by the blacksmith shop to borrow a horse to come out," he continued. "I can work there awhile to make some money to get us back on our feet."

"But where will you stay?" Katy inquired.

"I should be able to stay at the boarding house in town. Katy, you and Anna have been doing a good job looking after things here. I'll come out on Sundays after church. Spend the day with you all."

"That sounds fine with me," Anna said thoughtfully. I have no place to go. I like living here." She smiled coyly at Pa.

Chapter 18

Finally a new happier life began for the family. The routine was still the same. Katy did the chores and tended the garden. Anna, with Sarah's help, looked after the household duties. Anna took great pride in the little green sprouts near the house that would one day become beautiful flowers.

Sundays were always fun. After church, Pa came out to the farm. Everyone played cards or games. Anna fixed a big dinner. Jacob, a happy little toddler, soon got used to Pa. Raising his chubby hands up, "Pa?" he would question. He waited for the big man to lift him up and wrap him in a gentle hug.

~~~~~~~

The school year ended in June. A huge picnic for students, families and friends marked the event. The ladies brought sandwiches and sweets. Coffee and lemonade was available. Games were arranged: three legged race, potato on a spoon, London Bridge and B-I-N-G-O were a few of the favorites. Ring around a Rosie always kept the younger ones entertained. Finally teams were chosen for a ball game.

After the activities, a huge watermelon was split open. Everyone grabbed a chunk. They slurped the bright pink juicy delight. The boys decided it was great fun to spit the black seeds at anyone in sight. The girls shrieked and ran away.

Shouts of "see you next year" echoed around everywhere as people boarded their wagons or horses for the ride home.

~~~~~~~

There had been a long dry spell. The farmers were very worried their crops would be ruined. On Tuesday, the second week of July, black clouds started building. Forks of lightning clawed through the heavy sky. Thunder started cracking as though it would split the little house in two. Rebecca was more grown up and much calmer this year. She simply plugged her ears and buried her head in a pillow.

Before long heavy drops started pinging on the roof-top. Then a great torrent let loose, pounding heavily overhead. Two hours later the sky cleared. A light drizzle signalled the end of the storm. Katy struggled into her slicker and gum boots.

"I'm going out to check on the animals," she announced as she pushed the door open.

On a Saturday two weeks later, Katy drove the family wagon into town. They met Pa, Miss Holmes and the Bailey's there. It was time for the big summer country hoedown. The whole town joined in for a street dance. Oscar, Joe, Katy and Anna once again provided the music. Several times Pa came and asked Anna to dance. Katy noticed how happy Pa was. Anna's eyes lit up whenever Pa came by. Tommy asked Katy to dance a few times, too. The younger children chased each other. They wove in and out between the dancers.

By August Katy's garden was growling well. It was producing beans and peas. They ate some of the vegetables fresh and canned the rest. Anna's flowers were thriving. She finally had the colorful display she had dreamed about. The crops were doing well now, too. However by the end of August they were once again in need of rain.

Chapter 19

One day late in August Matthew Bailey raced into the blacksmith shop where Pa was working bending horseshoes over the hot fire.

"Mr. Robertson, you have to come fast!" he yelled excitedly.

"What's wrong, Matt. Slow down and tell me," he encouraged the young boy.

"There's a fire out at your place!"

Pa ran to the big horse standing in the corral outside. He jumped on her, not bothering with a saddle.

"C'mon girl, let's go," he commanded as he jabbed his heels into her ribs. Pa could see billows of smoke in the distance. He prodded the horse on to her fastest pace. Arriving at the farm, he saw part of the house was a pile of blackened ash. Flames were licking at the side of the barn. Sarah, Rebecca and Jacob were huddled off to the side, sobbing.

"Where are Katy and Anna?" Pa screamed before the horse came to a full halt.

"K-Katy went to free the animals," Sarah whimpered. "She didn't come back. Anna went to f-find her."

Pa grabbed a gunny sack and doused it in the water in the horse trough. He threw the sodden bag over his head. Shinnying low on his belly, he crawled into the barn. Through the smoky haze Pa saw a form sprawled face-down. Grabbing a foot, he pulled the body outside. Turning it over he saw it was Anna. Pa shook her.

"Anna! Anna, wake up!" he spoke sharply. She coughed and sputtered as she tried to breathe fresh air into her lungs.

"G-get Katy – think she's over close to the c-cow."

Pa covered his head with the wet bag again. He crawled on his hands and knees. It was so smoky inside, he couldn't see anything.

"Katy, Katy where are you?" he whispered hoarsely.

He thought he heard a low moan. Pa followed the sound and going by feel only, scrambled toward a still shape. His hand touched on a rubber boot. He dragged the motionless body by the legs across the straw covered floor. Finally backing out the doorway, more hands came to help.

"I've got her," Mr. Bailey said. Pa was choking from inhaling smoke. After a coughing spell, he started patting Katy on the back. Finally he heard a small gasp.

"Katy, try to take some breaths," he coaxed. Slowly, with Mr. Bailey's help, Katy moved her legs and arms sluggishly. She started to cough.

"Did the animals get out?" she croaked as she gulped in air.

"Yes, they did," Pa assured her. "You must've just gotten the rope off Bessy just before you passed out. You saved all of the animals, Katy. We almost lost you and Anna though," he said as a sob caught in his throat.

A few more men arrived on the scene. Heaving buckets of water, they were able to stop the flames from doing further damage to the barn.

Mr. Bailey hitched the horses to the wagon.

"Tommy will drive you over to our house. You can stay with us for a spell. Emma will be pleased to have the company."

The younger children scrambled into the wagon. Pa and Mr. Bailey helped Anna and Katy as they climbed onto the wagon. Katy leaned against the quilt she had thrown into the back of the wagon. She closed her stinging eyes and remembered back to the afternoon.

She and Anna, the girls and Jacob, had all been outside working in the garden. A sudden windstorm came up. Looking toward the house, they saw flames leaping through the window. Katy ran to the house. She opened the door. Fire was coming from the stovepipe. The draft from the wind blew flames through the open window. For some reason, Katy pulled the quilt off the rocking chair near the door as she passed by. Sarah was screaming that the flames were starting on the barn. Katy dropped the quilt in the wagon box as she ran toward the barn.

Katy knew she had to release the animals from their confinement where they were trapped. After she'd entered the barn, heavy black smoke engulfed her. From then on everything was vague. She groped her way to the stalls. She tried to unfasten the ropes holding the animals in place. Katy fumbled with the tightly knotted rope. She wasn't sure if she had set the animals free in time. Total darkness engulfed her as she slid to the floor.

Pa stood beside the wagon. There were unshed tears in his red rimmed eyes. "I am so happy you are all okay. We can build again. We can get new things in time," he continued. He looked at each one of them.

"I'll come and see you as soon as I can."

Chapter 20

As expected, Emma Bailey was delighted to have the family stay with her. The boys, Tommy and Matt, would bunk down in the barn for the time being. This would leave room for the girls and Jacob.

Mr. Bailey had gone to look at the damage at the Robertson's farm. When he returned home, he gave them a report.

"There's some good news," he said. "Part of the kitchen was pretty well destroyed because the fire started in the stove. The rest of the place has a bad smoke smell. But Anna's trunk was closed in the bedroom so everything in it was safe."

"What about the guitars?" Katy asked.

"I saw them setting against the wall in the living room," Mr. Bailey replied.

The following day, Katy and Anna took the wagon back to their place. They picked up some clothes for everyone. The guitars were packed to take along. Anna noticed the quilt was missing, but she didn't say anything.

The next Sunday, Pa went out to the Bailey place.

"A crew of men are coming next week to help fix up the house," he advised. "I was thinking maybe we'd make it a little bigger. Another bedroom. The kitchen could be larger." Why was Pa blushing, Katy wondered.

After supper Pa and Anna went for a walk. He seemed a little nervous. Pa cleared his throat.

"Anna," he said as he cupped her hands in his. "This might be kind of soon. When I saw you lying so still during the fire, it scared me. I realized I had strong feelings for you. I would like you to be part of this family."

He turned her to face him. "Would you do me the honor of marrying me?"

Anna's bright green eyes opened wide. Her mouth trembled slightly.

"I would be proud to be your wife, Charlie," she whispered softly. "I have become very attached to your family."

He wrapped his arms around her and kissed her gently.

"Let's go announce the good news," he laughed as they ran hand in hand toward the Bailey's house.

Chapter 21

The sun was shining brightly out of a clear blue sky on a Saturday in early October. Pa and Katy had completed the morning chores early. Katy and Sarah were putting decorations up in the new barn. The preparations had started a few weeks ago. Any spare time they had, the children colored paper that had been cut into heart shapes. Colorful bows were made from scraps of Anna's leftover material.

A couple of weeks ago, after harvesting was completed, the neighbors had helped construct the new barn. It wouldn't be used for housing the livestock until after the dance on this, Pa and Anna's wedding day. The animals had taken up temporary residence in the lean-to shelter in the pasture.

Anna and Sarah had been busy the last few days with food preparation. They were enjoying the new bigger kitchen. Mrs. Bailey came over whenever she could and helped out.

Rebecca was picking the few remaining wild flowers and some dried weeds to make arrangements for the tables Jacob was running on chubby little legs following his sister.

"Me, too," he muttered as he pulled some scraggly bits of grass as his offering.

"You sure are a big help, Jacob," Rebecca chuckled as she accepted his contribution. "You can pick some of those yellow leaves and we'll press them between pages in the Bible. They'll be pretty if we scatter them on the tables." Jacob grunted as he squatted down to do as his sister asked.

Around two o'clock teams of horses, pulling wagon loads of families, started arriving. Everyone was dressed in their Sunday finery. The women brought their dishes, cutlery and some food. Gifts were set out on several hay bales stacked near the house. Children of all ages jumped down and chased each other. They were happy to have someone to play with. Soon the preacher and his family arrived.

At 3:30 Oscar started playing a gentle waltz on his accordion. Pa and Anna were standing on the centre of the porch, facing the minister. Katy, Sarah, Rebecca and Jacob stood in a semi-circle around them. Pa was elegant in his Sunday suit. Anna looked beautiful in a long cream-colored dress, with lace trim around the neck and skirt bottom. She was holding a single flower from her beloved garden. Anna was sure it was a good omen as it was the only one that had escaped the frost. The three sisters were dressed in long, full-skirted floral dresses. Pa had bought the material in the summer with money he made working with the blacksmith. Anna has sewn them on Mrs. Bailey's old machine. Matching bows adorned their long, shiny hair. Little Jacob was handsome in his new overalls, with his blond hair slicked back.

"I now pronounce you husband and wife," the minister intoned. "You may kiss the bride."

The children giggled as Pa leaned over and kissed Anna.

Following the ceremony several people threw rice in the air above the wedding group. The little white pellets rained down on them, a symbol of good luck. Laughter and happy shouts rang out over the windswept prairie.

"Let's eat!" Pa shouted, as he led Anna over to the heavily burdened tables.

Soon, with supper over, the dishes were cleared away. It was time to open the gifts. People had very little money, so presents were very practical. Bowls and kitchen utensils, pillow slips and sheets made from sugar sacks, some embroidered with tiny stitches, homemade jams and jellies, even produce to be stored in the root cellar were presented to the happy couple.

Pa stood up and cleared his throat.

"I want to thank you all for coming to celebrate with us today. But mostly I want to thank you for helping my family this past year and a half. They couldn't have made it without you."

Uneasy with displays of emotion, the men looked down and shuffled their feet. Finally they started to clap and whistle their appreciation.

"Now, let's go to that big new barn you all helped build and have us a dance," Pa yelled above the din.

"WAIT!" Katy raised her arms above her head. "We have one more present for you and Anna, Pa."

The four children carried in a large basket covered with a towel. They placed it in front of the newlyweds. Slowly Anna lifted the material. Her mouth formed into an "O" and she let out a small gasp. She removed the article and shook it out.

"It's the quilt!" she whispered in shock. "I haven't seen it since the fire. I thought it had burned."

Katy had a guilty grin on her face. "I noticed it lying on the chair after the fire. I brought it out of the house and put it away for awhile. When you and Pa decided to get married, we thought it would be a perfect gift."

"Something looks different," Anna observed as she examined the quilt. Katy would barely contain her excitement. They had all been working on a new piece secretly for several weeks.

Anna spread the quilt out on the table. She noticed a colorful extension had been added to the top. She took a closer look. Tiny stitches formed a heart in the centre. Surrounding this were six stick people in various sizes.

"That's you and Pa and the four of us," Katy explained. "We're finally a family again. Our patchwork quilt is now complete."

Anna's piercing green eyes skimmed over the smiling faces in front of her, settling for a moment on each one.

"Katy, Sarah, Rebecca and Jacob, thank you very much. You couldn't have given us a more perfect gift. Tears spilled slowly onto her cheeks. She gathered the four children close.

"I am so happy you have made me part of your family." She smiled over at Pa who grinned back at her.

EPILOGUE

It was late September and the abundant crop had been harvested. A big party was being planned later today. It was Saturday and they would be celebrating Anna and Pa's 5th anniversary which was coming up soon.

Katy and Tommy were also announcing their engagement; they would be married in the spring when she turned 20 and him 22. Katy had gone to the city for a few months for training and was now teaching at the school. Tommy would be inheriting his parents' farm one day, so was working there on a share basis for the time being.

The last few years had been good for the family. Pa had slowly increased the cow population so he had a profitable cattle operation.

Pa and Anna had been productive as well, resulting in a set of twins born three years ago. Lizzie and Mark were active little toddlers now, keeping everyone amused and entertained with their antics.

The yard was cleaned and trimmed in preparation for the party later this afternoon. The younger children had made colorful chains out of crepe paper and strung them around the fence. Bouquets of wild flowers in jars were placed on the temporary tables. A huge WELCOME sign fluttered in the breeze. The main attraction as usual was the colorful patchwork quilt pinned to the clothesline. Of course two more little stick people had been added to it.

Katy, Anna and Mrs. Bailey were sitting on the porch watching the scene before them. They had been reminiscing about the past several years.

"Did you ever dream things would end up this way?" Mrs. Bailey asked Katy and Anna.

"Not in my wildest dreams," Katy chuckled. I guess I've learned something though. Life really is a patchwork design, isn't it? We certainly can't predict which way it will go."

Old Buster hobbled out and started barking. Horses, wagons and happy people were arriving heavily laden with food for all to feast on. It was time for the party to begin...

CPSIA information can be obtained at www.ICGtesting.com
Printed in the USA
BVOW071150261012

304046BV00001B/30/P